Horniman Primary S

This edition produced for The Book People Ltd, Hall Wood Avenue,
Haydock, St Helens, WA11 9UL

First published in hardback in Great Britain by HarperCollins Publishers Ltd in 1997
First published in Picture Lions in 2000
3 5 7 9 10 8 6 4
ISBN: 0 00 762437 9

Picture Lions is an imprint of the Children's Division, part of HarperCollins Publishers Ltd

The HarperCollins website address is: www.**fire**and**water**.com

Manufactured in China

ONE WARM FOX

NICK BUTTERWORTH

TED SMART

"Shoo! Go on, shoo!" said Percy the park keeper. "This isn't bird seed. Shoo!"

Percy was sowing some wild flower seed on a patch of bare earth. But a bunch of rooks who had suddenly appeared were trying to gobble up the seed as fast as Percy could scatter it.

"And you're not much help," said Percy to a rather saggy-looking scarecrow he had made. He sighed and tried to cover the last of the seed with his rake.

When Percy got back to his hut,
he found his friend the fox sitting
on the steps. Next to the fox there was
a parcel.

"Hello," said Percy. "I see
the postman has been."

Percy picked up the parcel and
looked at the writing.

"Oh dear," he said.

"What's the matter?" said the fox.
"Don't you like parcels?"

"Not from Auntie Joyce," said Percy.
"She knits things. This will be another
pullover or a scarf or something. I've
got a collection."

P ercy began to open the parcel.
    "She's very kind," said Percy, "but
somehow, the things she knits . . . well,
they don't really suit me. Not my sort
of colours. Either that or they don't fit."

"**P**erhaps they'd fit me," said the fox.
"I was a bit chilly last night."
Percy unwrapped the rest of the parcel.

"Well, this will keep your ears warm,"
he chuckled, and he tossed the fox a
woolly balaclava. "Very nice, but a bit
small for me, I think."

The fox pulled on the balaclava.
He looked a bit disappointed.
"I was thinking more of a pullover,"
he said. "This is squashing my ears."

P ercy smiled.
    "Follow me," he said.
"Pardon?" said the fox.

"I said follow me," Percy repeated
loudly, and he led the fox into his hut.

P ercy brought out an old suitcase from under his bed. He blew the dust off it and opened it.

"How about this?" Percy held up one of Auntie Joyce's pullovers. The fox put it on.

"It fits!" said the fox happily.

"So it does," said Percy with a chuckle.
"In that case, help yourself. I'm just
going to check my wild flower patch."

P ercy wasn't gone for long. As he
walked back towards his hut, he
didn't look too pleased.

But, as soon as Percy opened the door, his face changed.

"Everything fits!" said the fox. Percy roared with laughter.

"You can't go about like that!" he said. "Anyway, you'll be much too hot. You'll cook!"

"It is a bit warm," admitted the fox. "I just thought, at night, you know..."

"You can keep the pullover," said Percy, "but I think you should take off the rest. Besides, I think I know someone that these things might suit."

T he next morning, Percy was out
working in the park when he met
the fox again.

"How were you last night?" asked Percy.

"As warm as toast!" said the fox. "How is your wild flower patch? Are those rooks still being a nuisance?"

"I can't understand it," Percy chuckled.
"They haven't been near the place!"

Nick Butterworth was born in North London in 1946 and grew up in a sweet shop in Essex. He now lives in Suffolk with his wife Annette and their two children, Ben and Amanda.

The inspiration for the Percy the Park Keeper books came from Nick Butterworth's many walks through the local park with the family dog, Jake. The stories have sold over two million copies and are loved by children all around the world. Their popularity has led to the making of a stunning animated television series, now available on video from HIT Entertainment plc.

Read all the stories about Percy and his animal friends . . .

then enjoy the Percy activity books.

And don't forget you can now see Percy on video too!